Disney · PIXAR

THE WORLD OF

Cars

BACK ON TRACK

SCHOLASTIC INC.

New York   Toronto   London   Auckland   Sydney
Mexico City   New Delhi   Hong Kong   Buenos Aires

Everyone knows the story of famous race car Lightning McQueen's journey to the Piston Cup. But McQueen didn't do it alone. It took a very special pit crew who helped teach the hotshot rookie the meaning of teamwork. Here's how it happened . . .

This was it—the biggest race of the year! The white flag waved, signaling the final lap of the Piston Cup Series. Lightning McQueen and his rivals, The King and Chick Hicks, raced around the track dead even. All three sped across the finish line at the same time. It was a three-way tie!

To decide the official winner, the judges called for a rematch in California.

On his way to the tie-breaking race in California, McQueen became stranded in Radiator Springs. While there, McQueen worked hard and helped the town. Along the way, he made many wonderful new friends.

Soon it was time for McQueen to get back on the road towards California and the rematch. As he sped away, everyone in Radiator Springs was excited about his big race, but sad to see their new friend leave.

In his garage, Doc parked and thought about McQueen. He worried about the rookie trying to make it alone in the racing world against The King and especially Chick, who never played fair.

"McQueen just needs a good team behind him," thought Doc. "And someone to keep an eye out for Chick's dirty tricks."

CRASH!

The buzz in Radiator Springs was about who would win the rematch.

"Do you think McQueen can beat Chick Hicks?" asked Sally. "Chick is one mean race car."

"McQueen can beat anybody. I know it!" said Mater. McQueen and Mater had quickly become best friends.

McQueen's friends watched an interview on TV with Chick Hicks.

"McQueen? Why should I worry about him?" Chick asked. "He ended up in some rusty little town, tipping over tractors and taking Sunday drives. He isn't serious about winning. But I am!"

Doc almost popped a gasket.
"Listen up, everybody," he bellowed.
"The rookie needs our help. He's out there
with no pit crew and two tough opponents. I'm
not going to let Lightning McQueen lose just because
he thinks he can do it all on his own. Who's with me?"
Everyone was, of course! And they all had a job to do.
Luigi and Guido picked out tires. Sarge and Fillmore
gathered supplies. Flo prepared oil-to-go for the long drive.

McQueen's friends fell in line and headed to the race.
"There's the Interstate, Doc," Ramone pointed out when
he saw the smooth, wide ramp leading on to the freeway.
"We aren't taking the Interstate," Doc growled. "The old
road—the Mother Road—will get us to California just fine."

The journey was hot, long, and tiring.

At one point, a long row of parked trucks caught Flo's attention. "Look at that—a truck stop!" she announced. "Let's turn in, my tires are killing me."

Dozer's Truck Stop looked inviting. But Doc had a different idea. "Come on guys, we have to keep moving. No time to stop." And keep moving they did.

The crew grew exhausted by late afternoon. They were hot—and lost. They needed to find a place to spend the night and recharge their batteries.

Fillmore noticed something in the distance. "There's a town just over that ridge!" he shouted.

Everyone drove toward it with hopeful excitement.

The sun had set by the time they reached the town. To their disappointment, the little village was in bad shape.

"I don't like the looks of the place," Sheriff said, shining his headlights around. The town was abandoned.

"This trip was a mistake," a frustrated Doc announced abruptly. "We're lost. We're overheating. We shouldn't be spending our time going off to some fancy race. We need to get back home and take care of our own town so it doesn't end up like this."

"But, Doc," replied Mater. "McQueen needs me. He needs all of us!"

"You heard Doc. He knows best," said Sarge. "Move 'em out!"

As the sad group started back to Radiator Springs, something huge and bright suddenly floated overhead. It was a blimp—with a giant picture of Lightning McQueen glowing on its side! The line of cars practically jumped up and down with excitement.

RADIATOR SPRINGS

98 MILES

"Hey, do you know Lightning McQueen, too?" Mater called up to the blimp.

The cars from Radiator Springs didn't know how famous their friend was. But Al Oft, the Lightyear Blimp, knew. He agreed to show them the way to California and the big race.

Once again, the cars spun their wheels west, this time following Al. After a long night's journey, they reached the outskirts of Los Angeles.

"We're a long way from home but we're McQueen's family," Doc said to himself. "He needs us."

Indeed, the cars from Radiator Springs were a family—including McQueen. Doc, the head of the family, was glad they had made the journey.

By sunrise, the Radiator Springs crew was inside the stadium hard at work.

"Pit stop!" shouted Guido when he saw all the pitties and their tool racks. He rolled over to a spot to set up, while Sarge organized everyone else.

"Hey, Doc!" called Ramone. "Let me give you a paint job. You have to let these folks know that you're an important car—the Fabulous Hudson Hornet, a three-time Piston Cup winner."

"Not me," Doc grumbled. "Try snazzing up this pit instead. We need to show off our star car, not me."

Just then a red blur sped by on the track. It was Lightning McQueen!

Everyone from Radiator Springs pitched in to make McQueen's pit presentable. Mater and Flo searched for decorations for the crew to wear. They picked out red and yellow antenna balls to match McQueen.

"Looks like we're going to have a ball today, heh-heh!" Mater joked.

Meanwhile, Doc checked out the other crews. As he neared Chick Hicks's tent, Doc overheard something awful.

"I'm not going to let anyone get in the way of my winning that race today," Chick was saying to his crew. "If I have to, I'll make The King and that rookie wipe out so fast that their tires won't even spin. The Piston Cup is mine!"

Doc had to find McQueen and warn him about Chick's plans to run him off the track. "But can I find McQueen in time?" worried Doc.

It was hard to spot McQueen in the crowded pit row. Fans and reporters crowded around the rookie.

"Let's get closer," suggested Doc. But Doc and Mater couldn't get close at all.

"Give Mr. McQueen some room, folks," growled a big security SUV.

McQueen slipped away without Doc or Mater getting close to him.

Doc fretted. Had they come all this way for nothing?

Doc turned away sighing, frustrated that he couldn't get close to McQueen to tell him about Chick's evil plan.

Mater followed Doc. "Here, Doc, this is for you," he said, giving Doc one of the antenna balls. "You can use it to remember what a good friend McQueen is."

"You know what, Mater?" Doc asked. "We came here to do a job for a friend, and we're going to do it. Even if I can't warn him, I'm going to help him!"

"I think I could use that paint job now," Doc said to Ramone, when he returned to the pit.

As a high-octane boost rushed through him, Doc climbed the crew-chief platform and Ramone happily went to work. Number 51, the Fabulous Hudson Hornet, was back!

The race announcers spotted Doc and called out his return to the stadium audience. The crowd cheered.

"Look, it's the Hudson Hornet!" cried one fan.

Everywhere he turned, Doc saw a sea of flashing headlights. They were cheering for him! Doc was proud to be back, and it felt good to hear the crowd roaring its approval.

McQueen was thrilled when he found out Doc was his crew chief. With his Radiator Springs friends on his team, McQueen hit the gas.

McQueen drove his best race ever. But inches before the finish line, the rookie slammed on his brakes. He turned around and went back to help The King, whom Chick had rammed out of the race.

Although Chick Hicks won the race, no one cared. They were too busy cheering for McQueen as he helped The King limp across the finish line.

After the race, McQueen thanked his friends.

Doc smiled. "It's good to be back. I kind of like it up here!"

"Well, you had better get used to it, crew chief!" said McQueen. "'Cause there are a lot more races coming up!"

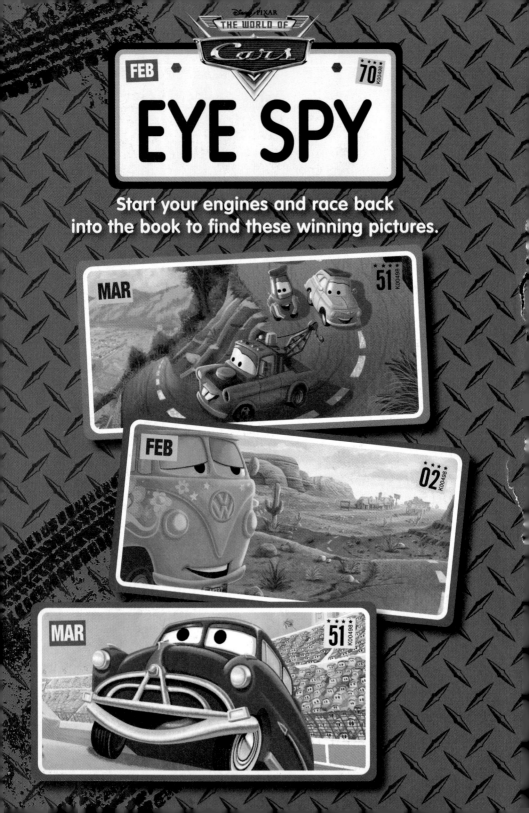